P9-AOZ-144

Shopkins™

Once you shop...You can't stop!

LOST AND HOUND

By Sydney Malone

SCHOLASTIC INC.

All rights reserved. Published by Scholastic Inc., *Publishers since 1920*. SCHOLASTIC and associated logos are trademarks and/or registered trademarks of Scholastic Inc.

The publisher does not have any control over and does not assume any responsibility for author or third-party websites or their content.

This book is a work of fiction. Names, characters, places, and incidents are either the product of the author's imagination or are used fictitiously, and any resemblance to actual persons, living or dead, business establishments, events, or locales is entirely coincidental.

ISBN 978-1-338-13554-1

10 9 8 7 6 5 4 3 2 1   17 18 19 20 21

Printed in the U.S.A.   132

First printing 2017

Book design by Erin McMahon

The Shopkins are playing fetch with Milk Bud.

"Who wants to go next?" asks Apple Blossom.

"Lippy, it is your turn," says Apple.
"I guess I could try," says Lippy Lips.
Lippy tries to throw the ball, but—*PLOP*.
It does not go very far.

"You just have to put some power into it," says Cheeky Chocolate.
But Cheeky puts *too* much power into her throw.

The ball flies into the woods.
Milk Bud runs after it.
The Shopkins have to find him!

The Shopkins head into the dark woods.

"Are you, like, sure you know where we're going?" asks Suzie Sundae.

"Cheeky knows the way home!" says Apple.

But Cheeky thought Apple knew the way out.

Now everyone is lost!

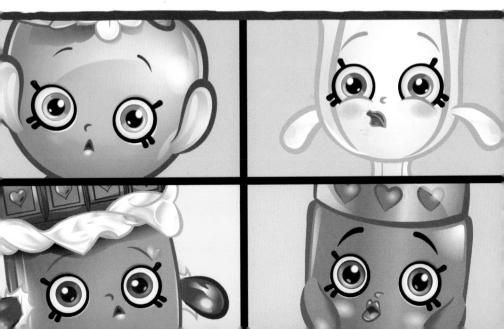

Lippy Lips is upset.

"I can't spend the night out here," cries Lippy. "I don't even have my lip gloss!"

Cheeky finds a shack where they can stay.
But it is small. There is not even room for
Lippy's extra shoes.

"Maybe we could get a hotel instead," says
Lippy.

Apple Blossom calls for Milk Bud.

"Where could he be?" she asks.

Then, Apple and Suzie hear a sound from the bushes.

It's Slick Breadstick!

"What are you doing here?" asks Apple.

"I am so glad to see you," he says. "I went for a jog in ze park and could not find my way home."

Apple and Suzie tell Slick about Milk Bud.
"I will help you find our furry friend," says
Slick.

Slick runs off to look for Milk Bud, too.

Then, Suzie finds a paw print on the ground. "Milk Bud must have been in the woods. We should stay here in case he comes back," Suzie tells Apple.

Apple takes a closer look at the paw print.
It looks too big to belong to Milk Bud.

Then, the Shopkins hear another sound from the bushes.

"I'm, like, way too scared out here," says Suzie.

Something jumps out of the woods!

"*Ahhhhhh!*" yell Suzie and Apple.

It is just Freda Fern. "We totally thought you were a monster," says Suzie.

The Shopkins tell Freda how Milk
Bud went missing.

"Now we're lost in the woods,"
Cheeky tells her.

Freda takes care of the park. She
knows the way home.

Freda also knows how to speed up the search for Milk Bud.

"I can give you a ride in my golf cart!" she says.

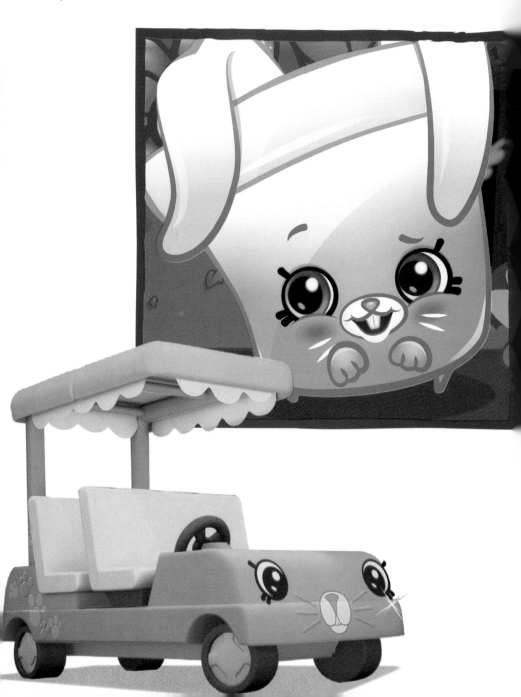

Freda Fern gives the Shopkins a ride back to Shopville.

Apple makes missing posters for Milk Bud on the way.

"Here is a map," says Freda. "You should start your search at the jewelry store."

Cheeky spots more paw prints on the ground.
The Shopkins are right on Milk Bud's tail!

Apple wants to hang up posters at the jewelry store.

Lippy wants to shop until she drops.
Then, Cheeky spots a charm machine.
"I want to be more charming!" she says.

Cheeky presses a button on the machine.
They have a small problem.
The machine makes the Shopkins shrink!

Cheeky, Kooky, Apple, and Lippy try to call for help.

They are so small that Suzie cannot hear them!

Apple looks at her map.
"Let's go to the Tech
Tower. I bet someone there
can help us," she says.

At the Tech Tower, Connie Console cannot hear the Shopkins, either.

"What ever will we do?" cries Lippy.

"Let's type a message for her!" says Apple.

Connie reads the message.

She knows how to make the friends big again.

"It is time to supersize some Shopkins!" says Connie.

She pulls a lever. The Shopkins are big again!

Then, Apple sees Milk Bud outside the Tech Tower!

She runs after him.

CRASH!

She runs right into Lola Roller Blade.

Apple starts to cry.

"I'm afraid Milk Bud is gone for good," she tells Lola. "I will miss playing fetch with him."

Lola has an idea.

"If Milk Bud likes playing fetch, you should look somewhere with lots of balls," she says.

Apple knows just where to go!

The Shopkins race to the sports center.
There is Milk Bud!
He has been looking for a new ball to
play fetch!

"Go long, Milk Bud!" says Cheeky.
Next time Milk Bud runs too far, the
Shopkins will know exactly where to find him.